WHY THIS IS AN EASY READER

- This story has been carefully written to keep the young reader's interest high.

- It is told in a simple, open style, with a strong rhythm that adds enjoyment both to reading aloud and silent reading.

- There is a very high percentage of words repeated. It is this skillful repetition which helps the child to read independently. Seeing words again and again, he "practices" the vocabulary he knows, and learns with ease the words that are new.

- Only 187 different words have been used, with plurals and root words counted once.

    122 words—more than three-fourths the total vocabulary—are used at least three times.

    80 words—almost half the total vocabulary—are used at least five times.

    Some words have been used 36, 37, 47 and 60 times.

ABOUT THIS STORY

- Trains are a basic interest of young children. This story can be used to encourage the sharing of experience with "rides," and leads naturally to the further study of transportation in the primary grades.

- There is a high repetition of phrases here which can be useful in combatting word-reading tendencies.

A TRAIN FOR TOMMY

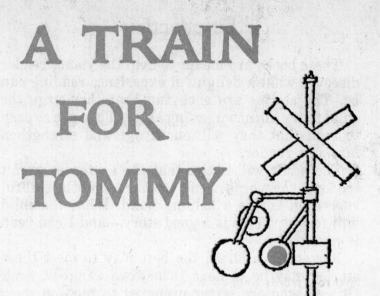

Story by EDITH TARCOV
Pictures by WILLIAM RUSSELL
Editorial Consultant: LILIAN MOORE

Wonder® Books
PRICE/STERN/SLOAN
Publishers, Inc., Los Angeles
1984

Introduction

These books are meant to help the young reader discover what a delightful experience reading can be. The stories are such fun that they urge the child to try his new reading skills. They are so easy to read that they will encourage and strengthen him as a reader.

The adult will notice that the sentences aren't too long, the words aren't too hard, and the skillful repetition is like a helping hand. What the child will feel is: "This is a good story—and I can read it myself!"

For some children, the best way to meet these stories may be to hear them read aloud at first. Others, who are better prepared to read on their own, may need a little help in the beginning—help that is best given freely. Youngsters who have more experience in reading alone—whether in first or second or third grade—will have the immediate joy of reading "all by myself."

These books have been planned to help all young readers grow—in their pleasure in books and in their power to read them.

Lilian Moore
Specialist in Reading
Formerly of Division of Instructional Research,
New York City Board of Education

Copyright © 1962, 1981 by Price/Stern/Sloan Publishers, Inc.
Published by Price/Stern/Sloan Publishers, Inc.
410 North La Cienega Boulevard, Los Angeles, California 90048

ISBN: 0-8431-4322-3
Wonder® Books is a trademark of Price/Stern/Sloan Publishers, Inc.

Tommy was playing with his train.

He was the trainman.

He made the train go

around and around.

The train went over the bridge,
around and around,
and into the tunnel.
The lights went
on and off,
on and off.

"Ring! Ring!"

Billy was at the door.

He was calling for Tommy.

Then he saw Tommy's train.

He saw the engine

stop and go,

stop and go.

"Say, that's a good engine!"
cried Billy.

It was.

Then Billy said, "Come on out
and play, Tommy."

10

"No," said Tommy. "Not now."

"Ring! Ring!"

Joe was at the door.

He was calling for Tommy, too.

Then he saw the train.

Around went the train.

"Whoo-ooh!" went the whistle.

"That's a good whistle!" said Joe.

It was.

Then Joe said,

"Come out and play!"

"No," said Tommy. "Not now."

"Ring!"

Now it was Judy at the door.

She was calling for Tommy.

She stood and looked at the train.

Tommy made the train go
over the bridge.
He made the lights go
on and off,
on and off.

"My, you do know about trains!"
said Judy.
"You must know all about trains."
Then Judy went away.

Tommy did know about trains.

He knew about engines,

and he knew about cars.

He knew what made them go

and what made them stop.

But there was one thing
Tommy did not know.
He did not know what it was like
to ride on a real train!

One day his mother said something
that made him very happy.
"Guess what?" she said.
"We are going on a trip!
We are going to see Grandma
on Sunday."

"Can we go on a train?"

asked Tommy.

"Maybe," said his mother.

"We will see."

But on Sunday

Tommy's mother said,

"We have to go by car, Tommy.

We have to take this big red chair

back to Grandma.

So we cannot go by train."

Tommy liked to go to Grandma's.

He liked to ride in the car, too.

"But I do wish we were going

by train," he thought.

21

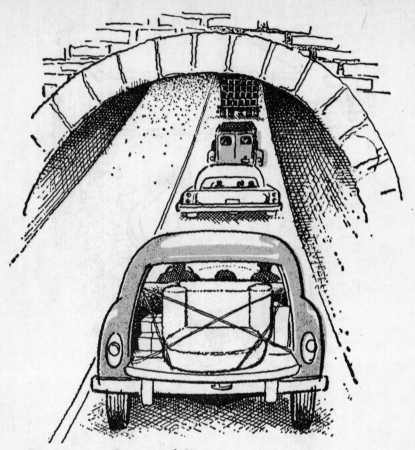

It was a long ride

to Grandma's house.

First they went into a tunnel.

"Wow!" cried Tommy.

"This is just like my train tunnel!"

Then they played "I see something."

"I see something red,"
Tommy's father said.

"Is it Grandma's chair?"
asked Tommy's mother.

Tommy looked out of the window
for something red.

"I see . . ." he said.

"Oh, look, a train—

way up there!"

Tommy's father laughed.

"If there is a train around

anywhere," he said,

"Tommy will see it!"

Tommy had a good time
at Grandma's.
Best of all, Uncle Bill was there.
"Guess what?" said Uncle Bill.
"I am coming to see you
next Sunday.
I will have a big surprise for you!"

"Tell me, tell me! What is it?"

asked Tommy.

"Tell me now, Uncle Bill."

Uncle Bill laughed.

"I will tell you this. . .

The surprise is—a ride!"

"A ride!" Tommy said.

He knew what he wanted

that ride to be!

Every day he said,

"I wish today was Sunday!"

And at last it *was* Sunday.

"Ring!"

Uncle Bill was at the door.

He was calling for Tommy.

"The surprise is here,"

said Uncle Bill.

"Come out and see!"

Tommy ran out to look.
There in the street
was a motorbike—
a shiny, red motorbike!

"Come on!" said Uncle Bill.

"I am taking you for a ride

on my new motorbike.

Let's go!"

What fun that ride was!

They went so fast,

the whole world seemed to rush by!

Then they went over a bridge.

"Wow!" cried Tommy.

"This is just like my train bridge!"

How fast the ride home was!

"Was it fun?"

asked Tommy's mother.

"Oh, yes," said Tommy.

"It was fun!

But, Mom, do you think that I

will ever ride on a train?"

"Some day, Tommy,"

said his mother.

"Some day you will.

Maybe the next time

we take a trip."

But the next time they went away,
they did not go by train.
What a surprise trip that was!

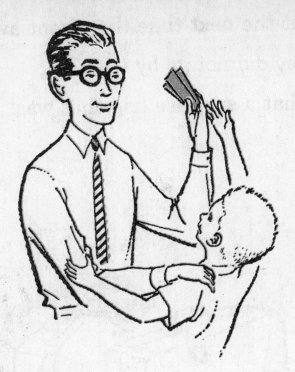

One day Tommy's father said,

"Guess what?

I have to go away on my job.

I have to go to the city

for a week.

And guess what this is?"

He held up something.

"Look!" he said.

"We are all going on this trip!

We are all going to the city—

by plane!"

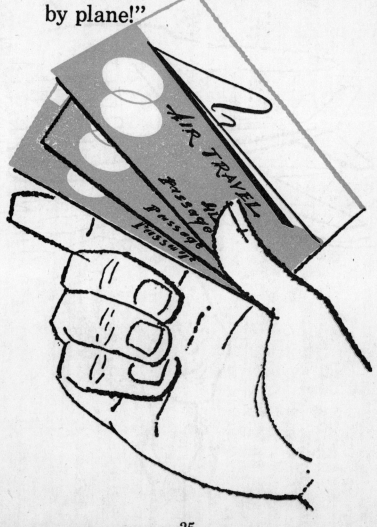

"By plane!" cried Tommy.

"When are we going?"

"In two days," said his father.

The next morning the bell went
"Ring! Ring! Ring!"
Billy and Judy and Joe
were at the door.

"Say, are you really going

on a plane?" Billy asked.

"On a real plane?"asked Judy.

"I wish I could go on a plane,"

said Joe. "Boy, you must be happy!"

Tommy *was* happy.
It was going to be fun
to go to a big city
in an airplane!

That night he put his trains away.

"I see trains go by," he thought.

"I hear them whistle in the night.

But do people ride in trains

any more?"

The next day, Tommy
and his father and his mother
went off on their trip.

They got to the plane
just in time.
They got in,
they got ready,
and the plane took off.

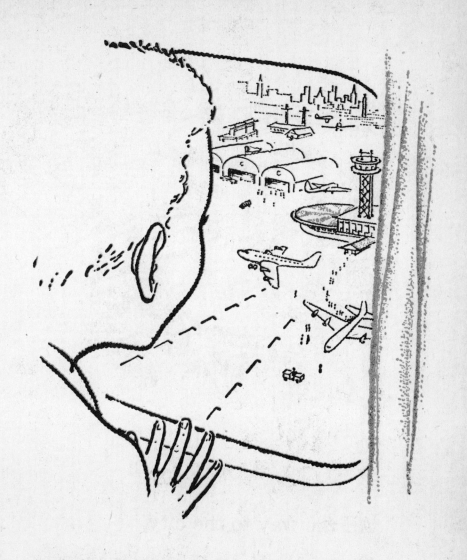

"Look," Tommy said. "Everything
is getting smaller and smaller!"

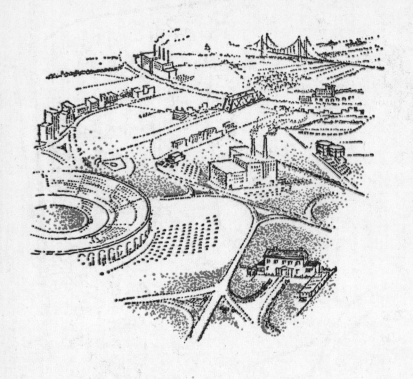

All the way to the city,

Tommy looked out of the window.

"Look!" he cried.

"Look down there! I see a train!

It looks just like my toy train!"

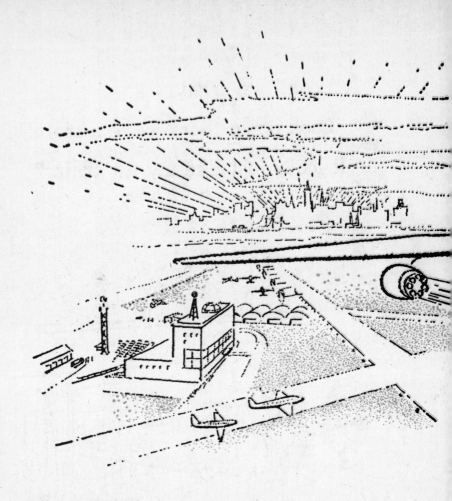

Then the plane came

        down,

            down,

                down.

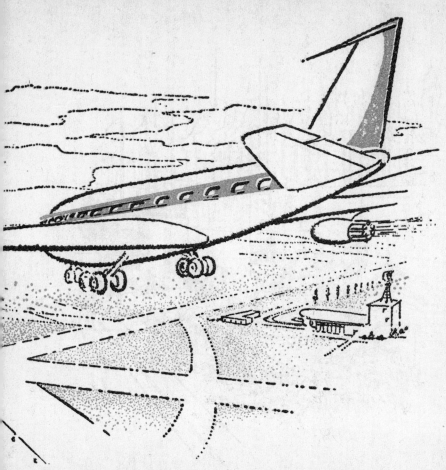

"Everything is getting bigger
and bigger," said Tommy.

Down,
            down,
                        down.
                                    Bump!

Soon they were right in the city.

Tommy's father had to work.

But Tommy and his mother

went here and there in the city.

There was so much to see.

There were so many places to go.

There was a surprise ride, too.

Then, all too soon,

it was time to go home.

That night they said good-by

to the city.

In the morning

they would take the plane home.

Tommy was the first one up
in the morning.
He looked out the window.

Where were all the houses?

Where were all the streets?

Where were all the cars

and the people?

Then his father

looked out the window, too.

"Oh, my, what a fog!" he said.

"I have never seen

a fog like this.

Will our plane go up today?"

Tommy's father called up
to find out.
"No," he said. "No planes
will take off in this fog."

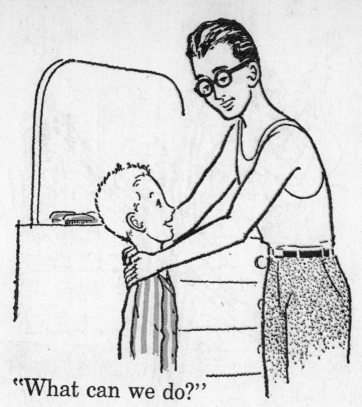

"What can we do?"
asked Tommy's mother.
"There is only one thing to do,"
said Tommy's father.
He looked at Tommy,
and he began to laugh.
Tommy began to laugh, too.

"I know! I know!" he cried.

"We are going to take a train!"

And they did.

At last Tommy got his ride

on a real train.

They took a long, long train,
with a big engine and many cars.
The train had its fog lights on.
"Whooo!" went the whistle
in the fog.

On and on went the train.
Then at last
they were out of the fog.
On and on went the train,
into a tunnel

and over a bridge.

How the world rushed by —

trees and houses

and people and farms!

Tommy was very happy.

"A train ride is best of all,"

he said.

"I knew it would be!

I knew it would be!"